WHO WANTS ONE?

WHO WANTS ONE?

Mary Serfozo

illustrated by Keiko Narahashi

Aladdin Books
Macmillan Publishing Company   New York
Maxwell Macmillan Canada   Toronto   Maxwell Macmillan International   New York   Oxford   Singapore   Sydney

For John

M.S.

For Micah and Peter

K.N.

First Aladdin Books edition 1992

Aladdin Books
Macmillan Publishing Company
866 Third Avenue
New York, NY 10022

Maxwell Macmillan Canada, Inc.
1200 Eglinton Avenue East
Suite 200
Don Mills, Ontario M3C 3N1

Macmillan Publishing Company is part of the Maxwell Communication Group of Companies.

Printed in Hong Kong
10 9 8 7 6 5 4 3 2 1

A hardcover edition of *Who Wants One?* is available from Margaret K. McElderry Books, Macmillan Publishing Company.

Library of Congress Cataloging-in-Publication Data

Serfozo, Mary.
    Who wants one? / Mary Serfozo ; illustrated by Keiko Narahashi. —
1st Aladdin Books ed.
        p.   cm.
    Summary: Rhyming text and illustrations introduce the numbers one through ten.
    ISBN 0-689-71642-7
    1. Counting—Juvenile literature.   [1. Counting.]   I. Narahashi, Keiko, ill.   II. Title.
[QA113.S47   1992]
513.2'11—dc20
[E]   92-4341

Who wants one?

1
Who wants one?
Do you want one?
One butterfly, one raisin bun,
One rainbow coming with the sun.
Do you want one?

YES, I WANT ONE!

2 Well, I like two.
Now won't two do?
Two shiny shoes, two kangaroos,
Two kangaroos in shiny shoes.
Do you want two?

NO, I WANT ONE!

3 Perhaps it's three
you want to see.
Three clocks, three socks, three locks, three keys,
Three treetops tossing in the breeze.
Do you want three?

NO, I WANT ONE!

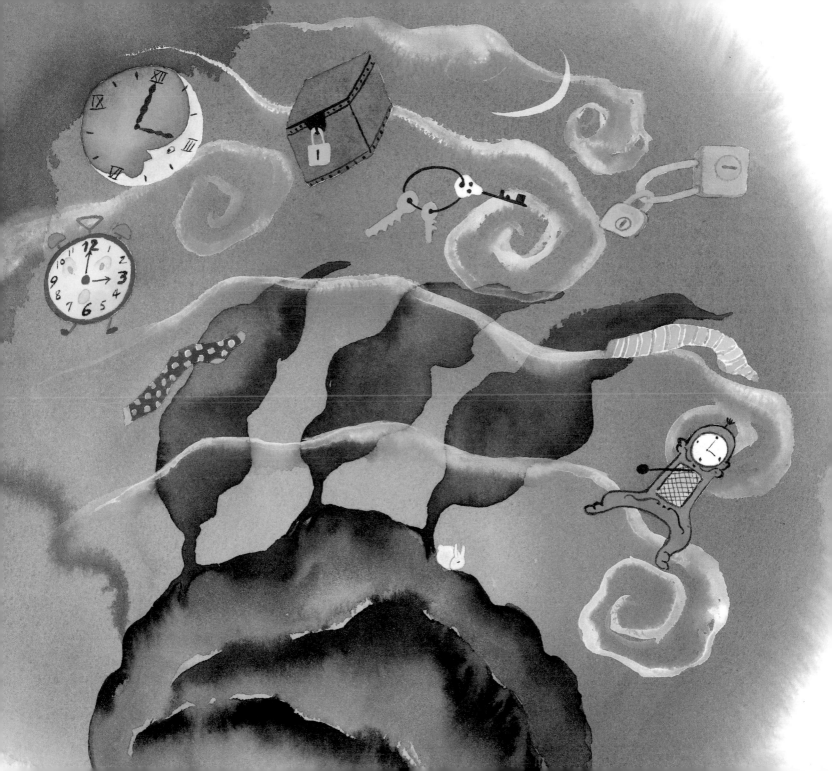

4 I know…it's four
you're waiting for!
Four goats in boats—just four, no more.
Four bright red boots beside the door.
Do you want four?

NO, I WANT ONE!

5 Or maybe five?
Well, sakes alive!
Five peacocks coming up the drive,
Five black bees buzzing 'round the hive.
Do you want five?

NO, I WANT ONE!

6

Do you pick six?
Look, here is six.
Six sails, six whales, six driftwood sticks,
Six jolly dolphins doing tricks.
Do you want six?

NO, I WANT ONE!

7 Then why not seven,
for heaven's sake?
Seven kites and seven cakes,
And seven swans on sky-blue lakes.
Do you want seven?

NO, I WANT ONE!

8 You might like eight.
I think eight's great.
Eight circus clowns all juggling plates,
Eight teddy bears on roller skates.
Do you want eight?

NO, I WANT ONE!

9 You don't want nine,
when nine's so fine?
Nine bluebirds sitting on a sign,
Nine green umbrellas in a line.
Do you want nine?

NO, I WANT ONE!

10 And now here's ten.
Do you want ten?
Ten speckled eggs from ten brown hens,
Ten pink pigs happy in their pens.
Do you want ten?

NO, I WANT ONE!

Well, now, let's just be sure…
We'll go back
and count again

all the numbers
from one to ten.

1 One

2 Two

3 Three

4 Four

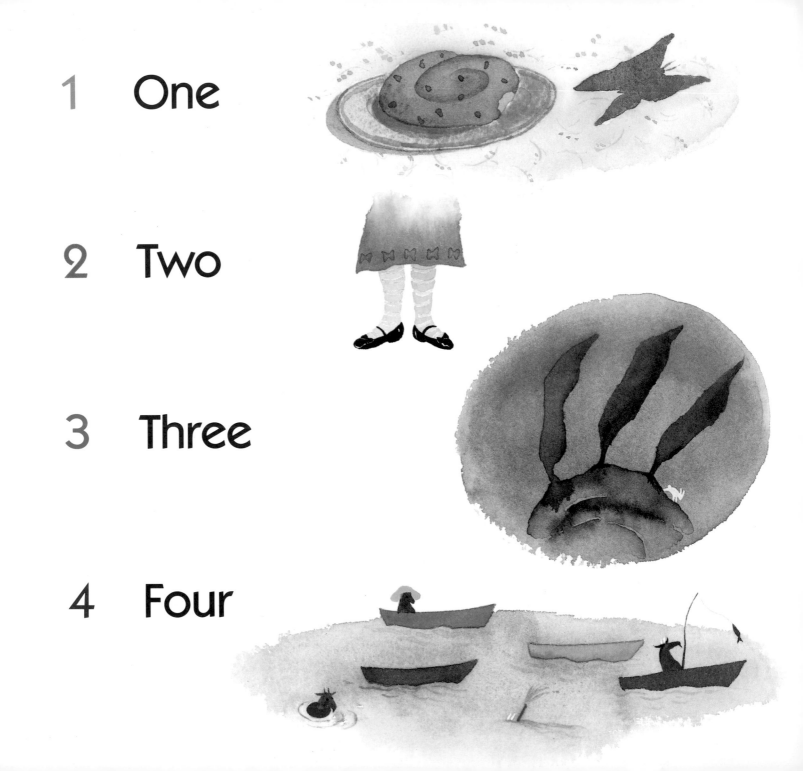

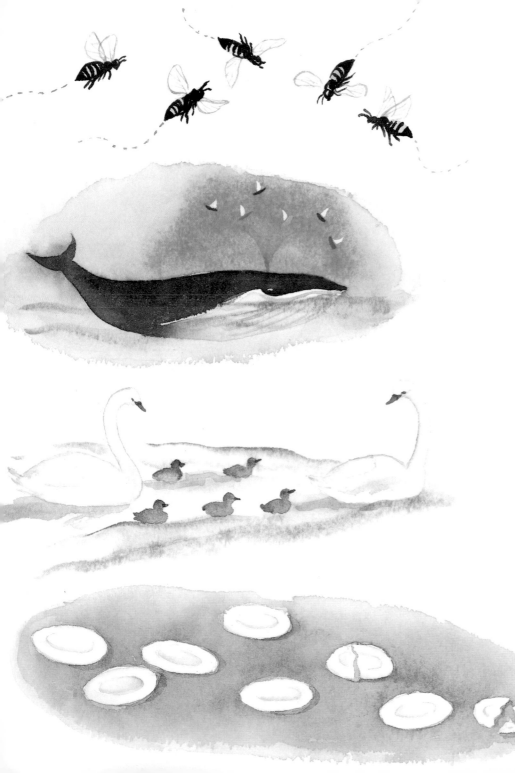

Five 5

Six 6

Seven 7

Eight 8

9 Nine

10 Ten

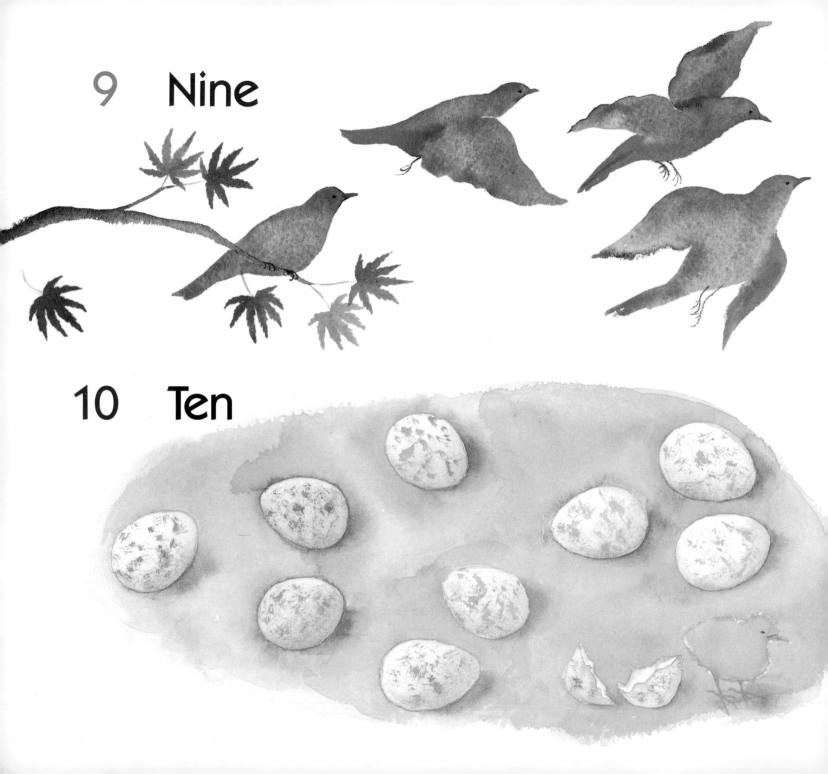

Tell me again,
now that we're done...

Do you want one?

YES, I WANT ONE!